TALENT SHOW TRICKS

Don't miss any of the cases in the Hardy Boys Clue Book series!

HARDY BOYS

→ Clue Book ←

#4

TALENT SHOW TRICKS

BY FRANKLIN W. DIXON ILLUSTRATED BY MATT DAVID

ALADDIN

NEW YORK   LONDON   TORONTO   SYDNEY   NEW DELHI

ALADDIN

An imprint of Simon & Schuster Children's Publishing Division
1230 Avenue of the Americas, New York, NY 10020
First Aladdin paperback edition December 2016
Text copyright © 2016 by Simon & Schuster, Inc.
Illustrations copyright © 2016 by Matt David
Also available in an Aladdin hardcover edition.
All rights reserved, including the right of reproduction in whole or in part in any form.
ALADDIN and related logo are registered trademarks of Simon & Schuster, Inc.
THE HARDY BOYS and colophons are registered trademarks of Simon & Schuster, Inc.
HARDY BOYS CLUE BOOK and colophons are trademarks of Simon & Schuster, Inc.
For information about special discounts for bulk purchases, please contact
Simon & Schuster Special Sales at 1-866-506-1949 or business@simonandschuster.com.
The Simon & Schuster Speakers Bureau can bring authors to your live event.
For more information or to book an event contact the Simon & Schuster Speakers Bureau
at 1-866-248-3049 or visit our website at www.simonspeakers.com.
Book designed by Karina Granda
The text of this book was set in Adobe Garamond Pro.
Manufactured in the United States of America 1116 OFF
2 4 6 8 10 9 7 5 3 1
Library of Congress Control Number 2016901232
ISBN 978-1-4814-5181-9 (hc)
ISBN 978-1-4814-5180-2 (pbk)
ISBN 978-1-4814-5182-6 (eBook)

CONTENTS

TALENT SHOW TRICKS

Chapter 1

OPENING ACT

Nine-year-old Frank Hardy sat in the school auditorium, going over a big checklist in a binder.

"Hey, Frank!" Chet Morton, Frank's best friend, waved from the stage. "Check this out!" Chet held up three microphones and pretended to juggle them. "Maybe I can be in the talent show too!"

Frank laughed. He'd been chosen as a Bayport Backstage Buddy member for the school's yearly talent show. That meant he was going to help with anything people needed during the show and make sure everything ran smoothly. He even had his own walkie-talkie to help him communicate with everyone around the auditorium. Mrs. Castle, the music and arts teacher who directed the show, said she picked Frank to work with her because he was so organized and reliable. He didn't want to let her or the students in the show down!

The kids in the show, including his eight-year-old brother, Joe, were in the restrooms, changing into their costumes. Rehearsal would start in just a few minutes. It was Monday, and the show was at the end of the week, so they had a lot of work to do!

Frank took a few moments to check in with the rest of the BBB crew. First he talked through the walkie-talkie with Eli Ramsay, who was helping to work the lights up in a booth above the stage, and made sure he was ready to go. Then he checked on Chet, who was at the back of the auditorium. Chet was going to help with the sound—making sure each act had the right music and making sure the microphones all worked.

"Hey, Chet," Frank called out. His friend was half-hidden behind a huge panel with all sorts of buttons and levers. "You ready to go?"

"You bet!" Chet said, flashing Frank a thumbs-up. "You know, this stuff is pretty cool. Maybe I'll be a sound designer someday. Or a DJ!"

Frank grinned. Chet was always picking up new hobbies. As he walked away from the sound booth, he grabbed the walkie-talkie that was clipped to his jeans.

"Come in, Speedy," he said.

The walkie-talkie crackled, and the voice of his friend Speedy Zermeño squawked over the line. "I'm hearing you loud and clear, Frank!"

"How are things looking back there?" he asked. Speedy was also helping backstage, making sure everyone was ready to go before their act.

"We're ready to go when you are!" Speedy said.

Now that he'd checked in with the crew, Frank looked around the auditorium to see if the student director had arrived yet. Olivia Shapiro was an eighth-grade drama student from Bayport Middle

School, which was just down the street. At that moment, Olivia and her seventh-grade assistant, Zoe, came sweeping into the auditorium. Olivia's face was red and both girls were out of breath. It looked like they both ran from the middle school. Plus, although it was a warm day outside, Olivia always insisted on wearing a scarf wrapped dramatically around her neck. Frank had heard her tell Zoe in a rehearsal last week that all the great directors wore scarves.

Olivia took her usual seat in the auditorium with Zoe beside her. Zoe handed her a bottle of water, a notebook, and a pen while Olivia fanned herself.

Frank went up to Olivia. "Everyone's ready to start."

"Thank you, Frank," she said. "Can you call the cast to the stage, please? I want to talk with them before we begin."

"Sure," Frank said. He got Speedy on the walkie-talkie and told her to send the cast out. Slowly, students started to trickle onto the stage. Most were dressed in colorful costumes or fancy clothes. Some held props, like Joe, who was clutching the half-dozen orange balls he juggled in his act. Others carried instruments, like the new kid at Bayport, Ezra Moore, who held his violin and bow.

"Attention, everyone!" Olivia said, waving her hand to get the cast's attention. "I have an announcement to make."

The students stopped their chattering and turned toward their student director.

"I want to remind all of you to have your friends and family book their tickets for Friday's show *now*," Olivia said. "You don't want them to end up without a seat, do you?"

The cast shook their heads.

"Please feel free to see me after today's rehearsal for more tickets if you need them," Mrs. Castle chimed in. She was watching from the back of the auditorium.

"Okay, then. You'll remind them tonight when you get home." Olivia clapped her hands. "Places, please!" Frank saw a few kids roll their eyes. Olivia could be pretty bossy, and not everyone liked that!

The students scattered into the wings at the sides of the stage. The first and last numbers of the evening were songs that Olivia had choreographed herself, and they featured everyone in the show. Frank took his usual place in a seat behind Olivia and Zoe and got out his walkie-talkie.

"Eli," he said. "Can you bring up the lights for the opening number?"

"Roger, boss!" Eli radioed back. The lights in the auditorium dimmed, while those on the stage brightened.

"Chet," Frank asked, "is the music for the opening number ready to go?"

"Whenever you are, Frank," Chet replied.

"Speedy," Frank said, "is everyone in position backstage?"

"We're ready!" she said.

Frank leaned forward to tell Olivia they were ready

to start, but she was deep in conversation with Zoe.

". . . think it's going to be okay," Zoe was saying to Olivia. "I heard Mrs. Castle say that over half the tickets have already been sold."

"*Okay* isn't good enough," Olivia said. "I want to be a professional director someday, and this is my first chance to prove myself. This show *has* to sell out. What happens if they take the show away from me? Then what will I do next year?"

"Um, Olivia?" Frank interrupted. "Everyone's ready to start when you are."

"I'm ready," Olivia said. "Let's go."

"Chet," Frank said into his walkie-talkie, "start the music. Eli, hit the lights. Here we go, everybody!"

Chapter 2

WARMING UP

When the opening number was over, Joe walked off the stage with a frown. He did not like to dance, but Olivia had him stepping and jumping and turning all over the stage in the first song, which featured the entire cast of the talent show. At least it was over for now!

Joe followed most of the other acts to Mr. Palmer's classroom, which was just across the hall from the entrance to the backstage. The talent show was using it as a greenroom, the place where acts not performing could hang out while they waited for their turn. Frank stood at the door with a walkie-talkie that connected him to Ellie Freeman. She'd let them know whenever it was time for them to get ready backstage before it was their turn to go on.

Joe sat down at a desk and took a swig from his water bottle. Then he grabbed his juggling balls from his backpack and practiced his routine in his head.

"What happens if you drop one?" Ezra asked as he sat down at the desk beside Joe. Ezra had only been going to Bayport Elementary for about a month. Joe knew him a little because he had recently joined Joe's baseball team, the Bandits.

Joe shrugged. "I just pick them all back up and try again."

Ezra played with the latch on his violin case. "I wish I had a cool talent like yours."

"The violin is cool!" Joe reassured him.

"I hate it," Ezra complained. "I mean, not the violin. I actually like the violin, but I hate the idea of everyone knowing that I play. Almost every school I've gone to, I've been teased for playing. I wish I could just keep it a secret."

Joe frowned. "Then . . . why are you doing the talent show?"

Ezra sighed. "My parents are making me."

"Oh," Joe said.

"Maybe I'll get a cold before Friday," Ezra said, "and I won't have to perform."

"Ezra, it won't be that bad!" Joe reassured his new friend.

"Or maybe the power will go out in the whole school," Ezra continued. "Or my violin will break. Or . . ."

Joe bumped Ezra's shoulder with his own. "Hey, don't worry. You like the violin, right?"

Ezra nodded.

"Then that's all that matters!" Joe said. "Besides, you play really well. No one will make fun of you when they hear how awesome you are."

Just then Adam Ackerman, the school's biggest bully, stuck his head into the greenroom.

"Hey, nerds!" he said. "How's your stupid show going?"

Joe just rolled his eyes, but he could see that Ezra was upset. He hadn't yet learned to ignore Adam the way most of them had.

"Keep moving, Adam," Ellie said. "What are you even doing here after school is out?"

"I bet he had detention," Joe said. A couple of kids giggled.

"As a matter of fact, I *did*. Detention's the only reason I'd hang out at this school after the bell. Not like you geeks." Adam cast his eyes over everyone in the room, looking for something else to make fun of. His eyes landed on Ezra and his violin case. He started to laugh. "You play the violin, Moore? Wow. And I actually thought you might be cool."

Ezra gave Joe a defeated look.

"Hey, leave him alone," Joe said.

"Yeah, Adam! We all know you're only jealous," Ellie added, "because when you auditioned for the show, Mrs. Castle wouldn't let you in."

A couple of people around the room gasped, while others laughed or hid their smiles. Joe wondered what Adam's talent had been. He'd have to ask Ellie later.

Adam's face turned red.

"Yeah, well, I hope your stupid talent show is a disaster!" he yelled.

Chapter
3

BUBBLE TROUBLE

At the beginning of rehearsal the next day, Olivia asked Frank to gather the cast. With the help of Speedy and Ellie, soon they had everyone on the stage, where Olivia was standing with Zoe and a boy who had a notebook in his hand and a pencil tucked behind his ear. Frank recognized him from the hallways, but he was a in a different class, so Frank didn't know his name.

"Attention, everyone!" Olivia said. When everyone

was looking at her, she motioned to the boy beside her with a flourish. "This is Diego Mendez. If you don't know him already, he's one of the writers for the school paper. He's here to write a very special article about the talent show. Let's give him a round of applause."

The cast clapped for Diego, who bowed his head.

"Diego, would you like to say a few words?" Olivia asked.

"Sure," he said, taking a step toward the group. "Thanks for letting me watch your rehearsal today! It's going to help me write a really great article about the show."

"We're going to be famous!" Joe exclaimed.

The cast laughed, and Frank shook his head. Joe loved to be the center of attention!

Olivia told everyone to get into their places for the opening number. After Frank told her everyone was ready to start, he went to the back of the auditorium. Olivia raised her hands and shouted "Action!" just like a movie director.

Frank looked down at the binder open in his lap. His job as the Backstage Buddy to the stage manager, Mrs. Castle, was to help keep everything from the lights and sound to the entrances and exits of the cast running smoothly. It was a big job, and he had every step of it written down in front of him.

He got on the walkie-talkie and told Eli to dim the lights in the audience and bring them up on the stage. Then he told Chet to start the music for the opening number. Once the music began, he radioed Speedy, who was in the wings, and had her send the dancers who were waiting there out onto the stage. The show had only started, and already Frank was nervous! There was a lot to do.

They ran through the first few acts, took a small break, and then went on with the rest of the show. Every now and then, when Frank had a moment to relax, he would sneak glances at Diego. He wondered what the older boy was writing about the show in his reporter's notebook. Olivia also seemed very curious. She was leaning so far forward in her chair to try to get a peek that she nearly fell out of her seat.

"Okay, Eli, turn on the spotlight," Frank said over the radio after the Connolly twins had finished their acrobatics routine. "Speedy, send Daniel out."

Daniel Tate, a fourth grader who was in the same class as Frank, walked out onto the stage. He stepped into the bright pool of the spotlight with his gold trumpet held in one hand. He lifted the instrument to his mouth to play "When the Saints Go Marching In" just the way he'd done at every other rehearsal, but Frank could tell something was wrong this time. Daniel blew and blew, but no sound came out of the trumpet.

Daniel frowned as he gave his trumpet a little shake. He put the trumpet up to his lips again, took a giant breath, and then blew with all his might. His cheeks puffed out and his face turned red, but no sound came out. . . .

Instead a stream of soapy bubbles exploded from the bell of the instrument!

For a moment, everyone just stared in shock. Then the auditorium went crazy. Frank could see

16 ⇌

Eli burst into laughter. Onstage, Daniel shook his trumpet some more and then tried to play it again, which made more bubbles come floating out of it. He started to laugh along with the others. Olivia screeched and bolted out of her seat.

"What is going on here?" she demanded. "Is this a joke, Daniel? The show is in three days, and I don't think this is funny!"

"It's not a joke!" Daniel said. "I swear! I don't know what's happening!"

"Frank!" Olivia barked. "Stop the show!"

Frank nodded and got on the radio. "Eli, turn on the lights in the auditorium."

As the lights rose around them, Olivia started to march down the aisle toward the stage with Zoe on her heels.

"Where are you going?" Frank called after them.

"I'm getting to the bottom of this!" Olivia said back over her shoulder.

Diego, who only minutes before had been slumped in his seat, looking a little bored, was scribbling furiously in his notebook as he jumped up to follow Olivia. Frank went after them and caught them onstage, where Olivia was questioning Daniel.

"You *swear* you didn't do this, Daniel?" she asked him.

"I swear on my favorite stack of Car Racer games!" Daniel said, holding up one hand. His eyes were wide and he looked a little nervous. "I warmed up before rehearsal started, and it was playing just fine."

"Could anyone else have messed with the trumpet between then and now?" Olivia asked. It was exactly the same question Frank would have asked. His father was a private investigator, and he'd taught Frank and Joe practically everything he knew.

"I don't know," Daniel said. "I put it back in its case before the opening number and got it out again just now. I guess someone could have done something to it in between."

"Where's the case?" Olivia asked.

"In the hall," Daniel said. "I'll show you."

He led them offstage, through the wings, and into the hallway just outside the auditorium. This was where a lot of kids in the cast had left their things because there wasn't enough space in the greenroom for everyone's stuff. Backpacks lined the hall, along with some books and stray props for the show. Most of the props were right off the wings backstage, but not all. Daniel led them to a brown rectangular case sitting between a blue gym bag and a pair of black tap shoes.

"Here it is," Daniel said. He opened the case.

Everyone gasped.

Inside was a bottle of Mr. Fantastic's Wonder Bubbles from Mr. Fun's Joke Shop, and a note:

This is just the beginning. I won't stop until the talent show is canceled!

Chapter 4

ON THE CASE

"Who do you think could have messed with Daniel's trumpet?" Joe asked. He and Frank were in the woods behind their house, on the way to their secret tree house. Their dad had built it for them, and it was perfectly hidden in the trees. You'd never see it if you didn't already know it was there. Joe grabbed the rope that was tucked behind the trunk of a tree and gave a tug, which released the hidden rope ladder. He and Frank climbed the ladder into the tree house.

"I don't know," Frank said, "but it looks like we have a case to solve!"

The tree house wasn't just a cool place to hang out. It was also the headquarters for Frank and Joe's investigations. It was their top-secret place where they looked over clues and talked over any theories they had on each case.

"We've got some pretty good clues already," Joe said. "Did you grab the note you found in the trumpet case?"

Frank pulled the piece of paper out of his pocket and handed it to Joe. "Sure did. Take a look."

Joe looked at the note, taking in every detail just like his father had taught him. The paper was from a school notebook, the edges frayed from being torn out. The words were written in pencil and in block letters that disguised the handwriting.

Joe stared at the note. He still couldn't believe it. Who would want to ruin the talent show?

A part of him was excited, though. He and Frank had been solving mysteries around Bayport for a while now, and Joe loved solving mysteries more than anything else. More than video games, macaroni and cheese, or even baseball!

"Once we found the note, Diego started asking a bunch of questions, and Mrs. Castle decided to cancel rehearsal for the afternoon," Frank said. "So, what do you think? Want to try to figure out who's behind this?"

"You bet I do!" Joe said.

They had a special notebook that they used to keep track of clues, theories, and the Five *W*s. The Five *W*s was a set of questions their father had taught them about. Finding the answers to the Five *W*s was the key to solving any mystery.

They started the way they always did, with Joe writing out the Five *W*s in the notebook in big letters:

The 5 Ws
1. Who?
2. What?
3. When?
4. Where?
5. Why?

"The *what* is Daniel Tate's trumpet," Frank said. "The *where* and *when* are at the talent show rehearsal in the auditorium this afternoon."

Joe wrote all that down. "So we just have to figure out *who* and *why*."

"I bet if we figured out the *why*, it would lead us to the *who*," Joe said.

"Good thinking," Frank replied. "Who has a reason to want the talent show canceled?"

"Well—" Joe started to say.

"Boys!" someone called. Joe recognized the voice as their father's.

Frank opened the trapdoor of the tree house. Fenton Hardy, one of the only people besides Frank and Joe who knew about the secret tree house, was standing below.

"Hey, Dad," Frank said. "What's up?"

"Chet and Iola are here to see you," he said.

"We'll be right there!" Joe said. Then he turned to his brother. "I guess we'll talk about this later."

Frank nodded. "Let's go."

They climbed down from the tree house and met

up with Chet and his younger sister, Iola, in their backyard. Iola was also involved in the talent show; she was going to be singing a song. Frank and Joe ended up doing almost everything with Chet and Iola, since Chet was their best friend and Iola was on the Bandits with them.

"Hey, guys!" Iola said with a wave. "Our parents said we could come over and play until dinner if you want."

"Sounds great!" Joe said. "Want to play kickball? We can do two-on-two."

"Sure!" Iola said.

"Pretty crazy about rehearsal today, huh?" Chet said. "Do you guys have any idea who it might have been?"

Frank shook his head. "Not yet, but we're going to try to find out."

"Whoever it was, they'd better watch out now that you two are on the case!" Iola said.

Joe got an inflatable ball from the shed, and they played Rock, Paper, Scissors to decide the teams. It was Joe and Chet versus Frank and Iola. Frank stood on home plate, and Chet rolled the ball at him. He gave it a huge kick that sent it soaring into the air. While Joe scrambled after the ball, Frank ran the bases, touching a hand to the swing set, the fence, and the biggest oak tree in the yard before running back to home plate. He and Iola high-fived. Their team was off to a great start! The lead changed hands between the two teams several times.

As the sun started to dip below the trees, everyone knew Chet and Iola would have to head home for dinner soon, so the game become even fiercer. It was the last inning, and Frank and Iola were in the lead by one run. Joe was on second base, and Chet was up. If Chet kicked a home run, he and Joe would win the game. Joe chewed on his lower lip nervously. Chet had never been a great athlete. While the others all played on the

Bandits baseball team, Chet had always preferred to pursue one of his ever-changing hobbies, from photography to model planes to computer programming.

As Frank rolled the ball toward Chet, Chet drew his foot back and let loose a monster of a kick. He connected, and the ball went flying over Frank's head. No one was more surprised than Chet, who just stared at the soaring ball in open-mouthed surprise.

Joe let out a whoop. "Run, Chet!" he cried as he started for third base.

Iola sprinted after the ball. Chet had kicked it far, but she was fast. Joe rounded third and sprinted on to home plate. They were tied! Chet was almost at second base. If he could make it home before Iola tagged him out, they would win!

Chet was running with all his might, and so was Iola. She scooped up the ball just as Chet laid a hand on the oak tree that was third base. He kept sprinting, headed for home plate, and Joe could see a triumphant smile starting to spread across his mouth. He was going to make it!

But then Joe saw Iola coming up behind Chet—*fast*. It was going to be close!

Chet lunged for home plate just as Iola lunged for him, touching the ball to his back. Chet threw his hands up in the air and cheered.

"I'm safe!" he said, jumping up and down. "We won!"

"No way!" Iola said. "I tagged you out."

Chet shook his head. "You tagged me *after* I touched the base."

Joe looked at his brother. He wasn't sure which one was right, and judging by Frank's shrug, Frank wasn't either.

"Don't be a sore loser, Chet," Iola teased. "I tagged you before you touched the base, and you know it!"

"I'm not the sore loser. *You* are," Chet said. "Why do you always have to be the best at everything, Iola? I won fair and square!"

"Nuh-uh!" Iola stomped her foot.

"You're being a baby about this." Chet looked down at his watch. "Come on, we have to go home."

Iola stomped out of the yard and back in the direction of their house.

Chet sighed. "Sorry, guys."

"That's okay," Joe said. He didn't like to see Chet and Iola fight. He and Frank hardly *ever* fought.

"I'll see you at school tomorrow," Chet said as he started to go after his sister. "Let me know if you need any help with your case!"

Chapter 5

BEWARE THE PHANTOM

"What's going on?" Frank said to his brother as they walked through the front doors of Bayport Elementary the next morning. The halls were full of kids standing around in groups, talking excitedly and all holding copies of the school newspaper.

Frank spotted Speedy in the hallway. Like everyone else, she was reading. He went up to her, Joe following behind him, and tapped her shoulder.

"Oh, hey, Frank!" she said. "Have you seen this?"

She handed him what she'd been reading. It was a copy of the *BES Gazette*, the school's newspaper. The headline was printed in big, bold letters:

THE PHANTOM OF THE TALENT SHOW: MYSTERY PRANKSTER STRIKES SCHOOL PRODUCTION

Frank quickly read Diego Mendez's article, while Joe leaned over his shoulder and read along with him.

Rehearsal for the annual Bayport Elementary Talent Show was going great. The musical numbers by the student director from Bayport Middle School, eighth grader Olivia Shapiro, have taken an already wonderful show to a new level. But nothing could prepare me for the, well, unusual performance of Daniel Tate on the trumpet.

Diego wrote about the bubbles bursting out of Daniel's trumpet and the hunt everyone had gone on to find the person behind the prank. Then he described the note they'd found in Daniel's instrument case, which promised more pranks if the talent show wasn't canceled.

Will the Phantom of the Talent Show strike again? All I know for sure is that I'll be watching, and you should too. Tickets to the show can be reserved on the school's website or by calling the head office. Better get yours soon!

Well, Frank thought, *that* part would make Olivia happy. She was desperate for the show to sell out.

"Who do you think the Phantom is?" Speedy asked. "You two must have a theory."

All around them Frank could hear other students asking one another the same question. Who could it be? Who would want to stop the talent show?

"Maybe it's Adam Ackerman," Speedy continued. "Ellie said he was hanging around rehearsal the other day, and he told her he hoped the show was a disaster."

"That's true. I heard him," Joe said. "He was really mad. Ellie said he tried out for the show but didn't make it."

"He did," Frank said. As part of his job as the Backstage Buddy to the stage manager, he had been at the auditions. "He came in and just joked around on the stage for a few minutes. Mrs. Castle said he could only be in the show if he prepared a real act. She offered him a second chance to audition, but he never came back."

"If anyone was going to do something as mean as trying to get the talent show canceled," Speedy said, "it would be Adam."

It was almost time for school to start, so everyone said good-bye and headed toward their classrooms. The Phantom was all that anyone could talk about all day. Adam Ackerman was the most popular suspect, probably because of his reputation as Bayport Elementary's biggest bully.

Joe told Frank he had a different idea, though.

"Adam does have a good reason to want the talent show canceled," Joe said as they sat down to eat lunch together, "but he's not the only one."

"Yeah?" Frank asked.

Joe nodded as he took a huge bite from the

PB&J sandwich their mom had packed for him. When he spoke again, the words were muddled by the peanut butter in his mouth. "I think the Phantom might be Ezra."

"Really?" Frank was surprised. He didn't know Ezra very well, but he seemed really cool. He didn't seem like the type of person who would try to ruin a talent show.

Joe nodded. "I know he's a lot nicer than Adam, but he's dreading the show. His parents are making him do it, and he's afraid he'll get made fun of once everyone knows he plays the violin. There's no one on the *planet* who would be happier if the show was canceled. Not even Adam Ackerman."

Frank thought about that while he took out the notebook to write their next suspect down.

"That does make sense," he said. "And it would have been a lot easier for Ezra to pour the bubbles in Daniel's trumpet, since he would have been in that area anyway. Everyone knows Adam isn't supposed to be there, so he would have had to be a lot sneakier to get it done without anyone noticing."

"We should talk to both of them and see if we can learn anything," Joe said.

Frank nodded. "I'll take Adam. You take Ezra."

"Deal."

After lunch, Frank spotted Adam in the hall as he was walking back to his classroom. It wasn't hard, since Adam was the biggest person in their grade and stood almost a head taller than everyone else. Frank ran to catch up with him.

"Hey, Adam!" he said.

Adam spun to face Frank, his usual scowl firmly in place.

"I'm not the Phantom, okay?" he said. "Whoever he is, I owe him a high five, but it's not me."

"Well, where *were* you yesterday afternoon?" Frank asked.

Adam crossed his arms over his chest. "Detention."

"So you were in the school after classes ended?" Frank asked. "While the rehearsal was going on?"

"Yes, but I didn't do anything," Adam said. "Not that I expect you to believe me."

Frank frowned. Adam had a good "why" to be the Phantom: he'd said he wanted the show to be a disaster. *Plus*, he'd been in the school when the bubbles were poured into Daniel's trumpet. But Frank had the feeling that Adam was telling the truth, so he wasn't sure what to believe.

If it wasn't Adam, could the culprit be Ezra?

Chapter 6

SOUR NOTES

Joe wasn't having any more luck cracking the case than Frank. Rehearsal had already started, and he still hadn't found a good way to ask Ezra if he was the Phantom.

"So, Ezra, did you read the article in the school paper?" Joe asked as they sat together in the green-room.

"Of course. It's all anyone's talked about today," Ezra said. "Pretty crazy, huh?"

"Yeah," Joe replied. "Did you see anything? In the hallway where Daniel left his trumpet case?"

Ezra shook his head. "I came straight here to the greenroom after the opening number. I was still here when Mrs. Castle canceled the rehearsal because of the Phantom."

"You didn't leave the greenroom during the break?" Joe asked.

Ezra shook his head.

Joe frowned. It sounded like Ezra had an alibi. If he was in the greenroom the whole time like he said, he *couldn't* be the Phantom.

"I'm going to go get a drink of water," Joe said. "I'll be right back."

On his way out of the classroom, Joe stopped to talk to Ellie Freeman, who was stationed at the door with her walkie-talkie.

"Hey, Ellie," he said.

"Hiya, Joe."

"Can I ask you a question?"

"Sure."

"Do you remember if Ezra left this room at all during yesterday's rehearsal?" Joe asked. "He says he was in here the whole time after the first number."

Ellie pursed her lips as she thought, but after a second she shrugged. "I'm really not sure. So many people come in and out that it's hard to keep track. Are you and Frank investigating this Phantom thing?"

"Just let me know if you remember anything weird about yesterday, would you?" Joe asked.

"You bet. I hope you figure out who it is!"

Joe walked into the hallway where Daniel had left his trumpet to check it out. It was a good spot for a prank, since it was usually empty during rehearsals. Joe decided he would walk from there to the backstage to see how long it would take. He needed all the information he could get if he was going to get to the bottom of this.

Joe walked from the spot the trumpet case had been toward the backstage at a normal pace, counting the seconds in his head. He went through the door to the backstage area and walked toward where Speedy stood just offstage. It was dark back there, the area lit by just one small blue lamp. He reached Speedy as she sent Iola out onto the stage for her song.

"Hi, Joe," Speedy whispered.

"Hey," he whispered back. "Mind if I watch for a minute?"

"No problem."

Joe peered around the black curtain that hid the backstage area from view. Iola was standing in the middle of the stage, a microphone in a stand placed in front of her. Her shoulders were thrown back in confidence, which made her look taller than she really was. The opening strains of her song, "Tomorrow," began to play. Iola took a deep breath and leaned into the microphone.

"The sun will come out . . . *RRRRRRRrrrribbit!*"

Iola jerked back from the microphone in shock. After a moment, she swallowed and opened her mouth again to sing.

"The . . . *Rrrrrrrribbit!*"

Once again, the frog sound croaked from the speakers. All of a sudden, the backstage area was full of kids who had heard the strange noise and come running to see what had happened. Onstage, Iola was moving her lips, but all anyone could hear was the croaking of a frog. Some kids were laughing, while others were whispering to one another that the Phantom had struck again.

Finally Iola ran offstage crying.

Joe heard Chet shout, "Iola! Wait!"

Then Olivia cried, "Stop the show! Everyone back to the greenroom!"

The kids backstage turned and scattered. Joe wasn't going to go back to the greenroom, though. He needed to investigate, so he stepped out onto the stage.

"What are you doing?" Speedy asked him.

"There's no way Iola could have been making those noises," he said. With Speedy at his side, he examined the microphone. It looked normal, but . . .

Joe tapped the mic. It made no sound.

"It isn't on?" Speedy asked.

Joe shook his head. He looked out into the auditorium and spotted Frank. He had to tell him this.

The stage was only a couple of feet off the ground, so Joe hopped down and headed for his brother. Frank was in the back of the auditorium in the sound area.

"Hey, Joe," Frank said when he saw his brother coming. "I'm starting to think this Phantom means business."

"I think you're right," Joe said. "The microphone on the stage isn't turned on. Wherever that croaking sound came from, it wasn't from Iola."

Frank frowned and went over to the sound equipment.

"Where's Chet?" Joe asked. Chet was in charge of running the sound for the show.

"He went after Iola when she ran away," Frank said. "He looked really worried."

Frank pressed a button and a CD tray slid open. Inside was a CD that was labeled *"Tomorrow" Music Track: Iola Morton*. Frank pushed the CD back in and let it play for a moment. There was no croaking. He pushed a couple of other buttons, and another CD tray opened.

He and Joe examined the CD that was in the second tray. It was a plain silver CD, and it had no label.

"Let's see what we've got," Frank said as he put the CD back into the player. He pressed play and the auditorium was filled with the sounds of "Tomorrow." The brothers looked at each other in confusion. Why were there two CDs with Iola's music track on them?

Then the croaking started.

"Someone made a copy of Iola's music and added croaking noises to it," Frank said. "They turned off the microphone so it would look like *she* was the one making the sound."

Joe didn't like what he was thinking. The music on the CDs, the microphone, all of that was part of the sound for the show. And the person in charge of the sound was . . .

Chet.

Chapter 7

FRIEND OR PHANTOM?

"I know what you're thinking," Frank said, "but it *couldn't* have been Chet. He would never try to ruin his sister's act . . . right?"

"It sure doesn't seem like Chet," Joe said, "but, well, they did get into that big fight yesterday. Maybe Chet was angrier than we thought."

Frank thought about that. If it were anyone else, it would seem like a good "why." But he had a hard time believing their friend could be the Phantom.

"Let's go find him," Frank said.

He and Joe searched the halls for Chet and eventually found him leaning against the wall outside the girls' restroom.

"Hey, Chet," Frank said. "Did you find Iola?"

Chet nodded. "I finally got her to stop crying, but she's pretty upset. She's washing her face."

"Poor Iola!" Joe said.

"She'll be okay. She's just embarrassed," Chet said, "and confused. She has no idea what happened."

"Well, we figured out that part, at least," Frank said. "Someone made a copy of her music that had croaking on it, and her microphone was turned off. It only *looked* like she was making those sounds."

Chet's eyes went wide. "Oh, man. I'm helping with the music and the microphones. I should have noticed something was wrong!"

"But . . ." Joe trailed off. He looked at Frank and then back at Chet. "But you didn't do anything, right?"

"Of course not!" Chet said, angry. "She's my *sister*.

I tease her a lot, but I would never try to mess up her act or the show!"

"We know you wouldn't," Frank said. He felt bad for suspecting Chet for even a second. Of course he wasn't the Phantom! "When Iola comes out, tell her we're going to find out who did this."

"Thanks, guys," Chet said. "Would you mind helping me with something else?"

"Sure, Chet," Frank said.

"Anything you want," Joe added.

"I want to do something nice for Iola," Chet explained. "Not just because of this, but because of that fight we had yesterday. She drives me crazy sometimes, but she's a really good sister. I have an idea that might make her feel better."

The next morning Frank, Joe, and Chet arrived at school early, long before any other students. Chet's backpack was full of their supplies, and Frank carried a white posterboard. They spent the rest of the time before school decorating a poster. They taped up sparkly letters that spelled out her name, pictures of her favorite band and baseball players cut from magazines, and little notes that said things like *Iola rocks!* and *We ♥ Iola*. They finished decorating the poster just as other students started to arrive. They hid around a corner holding the poster to see Iola's reaction when she discovered their surprise.

A couple of minutes later, Frank spotted Iola coming down the hall and elbowed the other boys. They grinned as they jumped out and saw her smile when she saw the decorated board.

"Surprise!" the boys cried.

"Oh, guys, this is awesome!" Iola gushed. "I love it!"

"It was Chet's idea," Frank said. "Joe and I just helped."

Iola gave Chet a big hug. "You're the best brother in the whole world."

Chet's cheeks turned pink, and he rubbed the back of his neck. "Well, I try."

"We're going to double- and triple-check your music today, Iola," Frank said. "The Phantom's not going to get you again. You're going to be great."

"Thanks, you guys," Iola said.

"Hey!"

They all turned their heads in the direction of the shriek that came from the other end of the hall. It was their friend Ellie Freeman. She was pointing at a poster for the talent show that was hung on the wall.

"Who did this?" Ellie demanded.

Frank and Joe rushed to check it out. Someone had scribbled all over the poster in a fat red marker.

Speedy ran up to them with another poster in her hand. It, too, had a note from the Phantom written on it.

"The Phantom did this to every poster in the whole school!" she said.

Frank turned to his brother. "We were the first ones in the school today," he said. "We would have seen someone messing with the posters."

Joe nodded. "Whoever it was, they must have done it yesterday after school."

"You're right," Frank said. "That means the Phantom is *definitely* someone involved with the talent show."

Chapter
8

A SLIMY SURPRISE

It was the final dress rehearsal. The talent show was the next night, and everyone was excited and nervous. The Phantom wanted to get the talent show canceled, and this rehearsal was his or her last chance. Everyone was holding their breath to see what the Phantom might do. Diego Mendez was there to see if the Phantom would strike again. The school paper was putting out a special issue on the talent show and the Phantom the next morning.

Olivia called the entire cast into the auditorium. She handed over her notes to Zoe—things like *Remember to smile* and *Keep your head up*—while she went to the restroom. While Zoe was reading, Joe snuck to the back of the auditorium, where Frank was going over his checklists.

"Hey, bro," he said. "I've been thinking."

"Oh yeah? Did it hurt?" Frank teased.

Joe smiled and rolled his eyes. "Ha-ha. Anyway, I was thinking I should hang out backstage during the rehearsal today instead of in the greenroom. If the Phantom tries something, I'll have a better chance of catching them."

Frank nodded. "That's a good idea. I'll tell Speedy you'll be back there."

Olivia returned, hands stuck in her pockets, just as Zoe finished reading her notes. Zoe tried to hand the notebook back to her, but Olivia shook her head.

"I want you to write down the notes for me today," she told Zoe. Then she turned to the cast. "Okay, everyone! Places for the start of the show, please!"

After performing in the first number with the rest of the cast, Joe took his spot backstage near Speedy while the other kids went to the green-room. From there he could see what was going on onstage as well as the table full of props that sat in the wings. The balls and fake rubber knives he was going to juggle were there, along with instruments, magic tricks, costume hats, and other items. No one would be able to mess with any of them without Joe seeing it.

Joe could tell that a lot of the kids were nervous as they went out onstage. As the show continued and there was no sign of the Phantom, everyone started to relax a little. Frank and the rest of the Backstage Buddy crew worked like a well-oiled machine, and even Olivia seemed happy with the way things were going. Joe's juggling act went perfectly; he didn't drop a single thing.

Annie Norland, Desiree Perry, and Lauren Brenner were the next-to-last act of the show. They were doing a dance number together. The three girls walked up to the props table where they kept the bowler hats they wore for most of their dance. The hats were hot and itchy, so they never put them on until the last minute.

"Break a leg!" Joe whispered as they got ready to go onstage.

All three girls turned and stared at him.

"Oops," he said. "That's probably not the right thing to say to dancers, is it?"

Annie grinned. "It's okay. We know what you meant."

Onstage, the lights went down.

"Okay, ladies," Speedy said. "Time to go!"

Annie, Desiree, and Lauren walked out onto the stage and struck a pose. The lights came up on them, their music started to play, and they began to dance. Joe wondered why the Phantom hadn't struck that day. Maybe whoever it was had given up, or maybe they hadn't been able to perform their prank because of Joe standing guard over the props table.

Joe watched the girls dancing. If he had to guess, he'd bet they were going to be the crowd favorite. His favorite part of their act was coming up: the moment when they took off their hats and shook out their hair as the music got really loud and crazy. Joe inched closer to the stage so he'd have a better view.

The girls took off their hats, and Desiree shook out her long black hair while Lauren whipped her auburn curls around her face. But when Annie spun, instead of her blond hair flying behind her, huge globs of green slime started going everywhere!

Onstage, Desiree caught a glimpse of Annie's hair and shrieked. Lauren froze and stared at her friend.

"Stop!" Olivia shouted over the music. "Stop the show!"

"What is it?" Annie asked, looking at her dumbstruck friends.

"Annie, your—your hair!" Desiree stammered, pointing to her friend's head.

Annie grabbed a handful of her hair and held it up to her eyes. When she saw the electric green color, she screamed.

"What *is* that?" she screeched. "Get it out of my hair!"

Joe rushed onto the stage just as Annie rushed off, followed by her friends. He gathered up the hats the girls had dropped and was already examining them when Frank got there. One of the hats had a layer of thick green slime smeared on the inside of it.

"Someone put that green goop in the hat," Joe explained to Frank, showing him what he'd found. "I don't know how they did it. I was backstage next to the prop table the entire time."

"The Phantom must have done it before you started standing there," Frank said. "Either that, or the person who's doing this really *is* a phantom."

Olivia appeared on the stage, with Zoe and Diego following her. Diego's pencil was flying across his notebook. He would sure have an interesting story for tomorrow's special edition of the paper!

"Frank, get everyone on the stage, please," Olivia said. "I need to talk to them."

Frank got on the radio to give the message to the backstage crew, and together they gathered the cast onstage. The last people to arrive were Annie, Desiree, and Lauren. Annie had been trying to wash the slime out of her hair in the girls' restroom with her friends' help. Her wet hair was dripping water down the back of her costume, and it still looked pretty green to Joe.

"This was stuck to the bathroom mirror," she told everyone. Annie held up a small piece of paper. "It says 'Cancel the talent show or this won't be the last you hear from me. Love, the Phantom.'"

Chapter 9

IN THE SPOTLIGHT

It was Friday, and almost time for the show to begin. The auditorium was packed with people. Not only was every seat sold out, but there was a row of people standing in the back. The entire school had turned up to see the show because of Diego's articles about the Phantom.

Olivia was the happiest Frank had ever seen her. The two of them were overseeing last-minute preparations backstage. Frank was dressed all in black, just like the rest of the Backstage Buddy crew, while Olivia was wearing a sparkly pink dress with elbow-length white gloves. Frank thought it was weird that Olivia was wearing the long gloves, but then again, most of the things Olivia wore seemed weird to Frank!

"This is extraordinary, Olivia," Mrs. Castle said. "I've never seen so many people in the audience for the talent show!"

Olivia beamed. "Thank you, Mrs. Castle."

Frank felt a tap on his shoulder and turned to find Speedy standing next to him.

"We have a problem, boss," she said. "Olivia should probably come too."

Frank grabbed Olivia, and the two of them followed Speedy to the greenroom where the cast, in lots of colorful costumes, was waiting for the show to begin.

"What's going on?" Olivia asked.

"They're scared," Speedy said. "They don't want to do the show."

A boy in a tuxedo jacket and top hat said, "What if the Phantom does something?"

A girl in a silver leotard who had her arm around her friend nodded. "Yeah, what if the Phantom makes something go wrong with my act and everyone out there laughs at me?"

"We should just cancel the show like the Phantom says," someone else shouted.

More and more kids started to chime in, until the room was full of noise. Olivia tried to shush them, but no one could hear her over all the talking. Finally, she stood on a chair, stuck two fingers in her mouth, and let out an ear-piercing whistle that made everyone freeze.

"Listen up, everybody!" Olivia said. "There's a saying in show business: 'The show must go on.' If we cancel the talent show, the Phantom wins. Does anyone want that?"

Everyone in the cast shook their heads.

"You all are too talented and you've worked too hard to give up now," she continued. "The only way we can beat the Phantom is by going ahead with the show and doing the best job we can. Right?"

The kids looked at one another and started to nod.

"This auditorium is packed with people who want to see you perform, and I know we can give them an *amazing* show," Olivia said. She pointed at the boy in the tuxedo and top hat. "Will, don't you want your classmates to see how great you are at magic?"

Will nodded. "Yeah."

"And Iola," Olivia said. "Don't you want your parents to hear you sing?" Iola stood. "You bet I do!"

"You're all going to be incredible tonight," Olivia said, "so let's get out there and give that audience the best show they've ever seen!"

"Yeah!" the cast cheered.

"Great!" Olivia said. "Now, get to your places for the opening number, and let's have a great show!"

The cast gave each other high fives and pats on the back as they walked to their places. Frank stayed behind to talk to Speedy for a minute, and when he headed toward the auditorium to take his place, he spotted Ezra Moore talking to Olivia. Ezra was one of Joe's top suspects, so Frank walked extra slowly past the two of them and kept his ears open.

"Please, Olivia," Ezra said. "Don't make me go out there."

"You're going to do this, Ezra," Olivia said. "I've done *everything* I could to make this the best talent show ever, and you're not going to ruin it for me."

Frank's attention was so focused on listening to the conversation that he didn't notice Annie Norland until he bumped right into her.

"Oops! Sorry, Annie!" he said.

"That's okay," she said. "No harm done."

"Hey," he added, looking at the long blond hair falling over her shoulders. "It looks like all the green came out of your hair!"

She laughed. "Yeah, I only had to wash it seven times. Look at this, though." She bent down to show him the top of her head. The skin beneath her hair was still pretty green. "It came out of my hair, but I guess the color in that slime takes longer to wash off skin."

"Well, at least no one can see it," Frank said. "Make sure you check your hat before you put it on tonight, okay?"

She smiled. "You bet I will. Have a good show, Frank."

"You too," Frank said.

He made his way to the small desk that Mrs. Castle had set up for him in the back of the auditorium. It had a tiny reading light that he could use to read his checklists and his notebook, where he'd written down all the instructions for the show.

Frank's heart was beating fast in his chest from excitement and a little bit of nervousness. He wasn't thinking about the Phantom anymore, just the job in front of him.

Frank got on the radio and checked in with the crew. Speedy told him that everyone was in place backstage and ready to go. Chet and Eli both assured him that they were ready with the right music and lights. Soon after, Olivia came to check in with him.

"Are we ready?" she asked. "It's almost time."

"We're ready when you are," he said.

"I want to thank you, Frank. You've been an excellent BBB stage manager." She gave him her gloved hand to shake. "I'm sure you're going to do a great job tonight."

"Thanks, Olivia," he said. He found himself staring at those odd elbow-length gloves Olivia was wearing as he shook her hand.

"Okay, Frank," she said. "Start the show."

Frank nodded and got on the radio. "Here we go, everybody!"

The lights went down in the auditorium, and

the sold-out audience began to clap and cheer as the curtain rose and the music swelled. Kids spilled onto the stage. The show had started. Olivia clapped her gloved hands in excitement next to Frank.

All of a sudden, it hit Frank like a bolt of lightning.

He knew who the Phantom was!

Do you?

THE HARDY BOYS—and
YOU!

CAN YOU SOLVE THE MYSTERY OF THE TALENT SHOW TRICKS?

Grab a piece of paper and write your answers down.
Or just turn the page to find out!

1. Frank and Joe came up with a list of suspects.
   Can you think of more? Who do you think
   is playing the tricks on the talent show acts?

2. Which clues helped you to solve this mystery?
   Write them down.

Chapter 10

THE GRAND FINALE

Joe and the rest of the cast ran off the stage with giant grins on their faces. The show had just ended, and it had gone perfectly. All their hard work in rehearsals had paid off, and they'd gotten a huge standing ovation from the sold-out audience. Even better than that, there'd been no sign of the Phantom.

Everyone hugged and gave each other high fives back in the greenroom. Joe stood up on a chair and shouted above the noise. "Hey, everybody! You were all awesome tonight! We pulled it off!"

The entire cast cheered, and the kids standing next to Ezra patted him on the back. A smile slowly spread across his face, and soon he was beaming more than anyone else. He had made it through the show!

Joe climbed down from the chair and went up to him. "You were great, Ezra. There's no *way* anyone's going to make fun of you after that."

Ezra nodded. "Thanks, Joe."

Joe went to where he'd left his backpack against the wall and started to put away his juggling props. He was zipping the bag closed when he felt a hand on his shoulder. He turned and found Frank standing there.

"Hey!" he said. "Good job tonight!"

"Thanks! You were great too. You didn't drop a single ball. I'm impressed," Frank joked.

"And *you* managed to keep the lights on for the whole show," Joe teased back.

"Listen." Frank stepped close to him and

dropped his voice low. "I think I know who the Phantom is."

"Really?" Joe said.

"Yeah. I was talking to Annie and—"

"Congratulations, ladies and gentlemen!" Olivia said as she and Mrs. Castle entered the greenroom together. "You were magnificent!"

"Yes, excellent job, everyone," Mrs. Castle said. "As a reward for all your hard work, we have a little surprise for you. Pizza party in the music room!"

Everyone cheered and followed Mrs. Castle to her classroom. Boxes of all kinds of pizza, bottles of soda, and a plate full of cupcakes were waiting for them. Joe ran to get a plate before all the pepperoni was gone. He sat down with Speedy, Chet, and Iola and dug into his slice.

It wasn't until Frank sat down beside him that Joe remembered. The Phantom! The idea of pizza had completely made him forget that his brother thought he knew who the Phantom was. He must have been even hungrier than usual.

Joe nudged his brother. "So, about what you were saying before?"

"Oh, right," Frank said. "Well, there's just one thing I need to check before I'm completely, one hundred percent sure. Hand me your cup."

Joe handed over his empty plastic cup and watched his brother as he stood and walked to the table of soda bottles. He poured a full cup of cola and started to walk back. Halfway there, he tripped over his own feet and "accidentally" poured the cup of soda all over Olivia.

"Ahhhhh!" Olivia squealed. "Watch what you're doing!"

"Oops!" Frank said. "I'm sorry!"

Zoe ran to get a stack of napkins and started to dab at Olivia's white gloves, which were covered with the brown cola.

"It'll be okay!" Zoe said. "Take these gloves off, and I'll go wash them in the sink."

"No, it's fine," Olivia said quickly. "Don't worry about it."

"Don't be silly," Zoe insisted. "You're going to be all wet and sticky."

"I don't mind!" Olivia snapped.

"It will only take a minute!" Zoe said, and she pulled off one of Olivia's long gloves.

Joe stared.

Olivia's hands were stained a bright neon green.

"Hey," Annie said, looking up from her conversation with Desiree and Lauren. "Olivia, why are your fingers green?"

"What?" Olivia stammered. "I—uh—I don't—"

She tried to hide her hand, but her dress didn't have any pockets. It was too late anyway. Too many people had already seen her green fingers.

"Your fingers!" Annie exclaimed, jumping to her feet. "They're stained the same color as that slime the Phantom put in my hat!"

Olivia's face was pale.

"Wait—are *you* the Phantom?" Annie asked.

"Olivia," Mrs. Castle asked, a worried expression on her face. "What's going on here?"

"Okay, fine, it was me!" Olivia burst out. She pointed at Annie. "I put that stupid green gooey stuff in your hat and put the bubbles in Daniel's trumpet and made it seem like Iola was croaking! But I did it for all of *you*. I just wanted this to be the biggest, best talent show ever, and . . . and . . ."

"And you knew that articles in the school newspaper about the 'Phantom of the Talent Show' would get the whole school excited for the show," Frank finished. "You were scared that tickets weren't selling fast enough, and you needed to do something to make sure the show was a success."

"It worked, didn't it?" Olivia pointed out. "That was the biggest audience the talent show has ever had!"

Mrs. Castle shook her head. "Olivia, you should have known better," she scolded. "That's not the mark of a good director!"

Olivia looked down at the floor.

"I'm sorry, guys," she said softly. "I didn't mean to scare anyone or ruin your hair, Annie! I just wanted people to see our show."

Annie's frown slowly disappeared, and she sighed. "Well, the green is already washing out. I'm still kind of mad, but I forgive you, Olivia."

"Yeah, me too," Daniel said.

"And me," Iola piped up.

Olivia gave Annie a big hug. "Oh, thank you. I really am sorry. I know I got carried away this time. Mrs. Castle, I'll accept whatever punishment you think I deserve."

Mrs. Castle put a hand on Olivia's shoulder. "We can talk about that on Monday. For now, let's all just enjoy the party."

The cast and crew finished their pizza and cupcakes, and then they all waved good-bye to one another as they went home with their parents.

"I can't believe Olivia did that," Frank said. He and Joe were heading out to their tree house after the party.

"She was always a little dramatic, but I didn't

think she would try to ruin the show," Joe added. "At least she was sorry about everything."

The boys climbed up to the tree house, using their flashlights to guide the way.

With big grins, Joe and Frank gave each other a high five as they settled in for a fun tree house sleepover.

"Rawwwr!"

Frank Hardy jumped nearly a foot in the air, splashing the milk from his cereal bowl all over his brand-new navy-blue T-shirt. "Joe! That's not funny!"

"It's not?" Eight-year-old Joe Hardy disagreed. In fact, he was laughing so hard, he thought orange juice would come out his nose. "Don't worry, Frank. I know I do a killer bear impression, but it's just me." He laughed some more while his brother grumbled under his breath.

"Joe Hardy!"

Joe's laughter died in his throat as soon as he heard his father, Fenton Hardy, shout his name.

"Stop teasing your brother," Mr. Hardy said, peering at Joe over his newspaper. But Joe thought he saw a smile in his father's eyes.

Frank refilled his bowl of Healthy Nut Crunch with fresh milk and took a seat back at the breakfast table with Joe and Mr. Hardy.

"I'm not teasing Frank," explained Joe, slurping the sweet milk from his bowl of Sugar-O's. "I'm helping him face his fears."

"I'm not afraid!" said Frank. But when he looked at his watch and saw that he would be at Bayport Bear Park, along with the other third and fourth graders, in less than an hour, he shivered.

In his nine years, Frank had faced a lot of fears solving mysteries with his younger brother, Joe, and their friends—their dad had even built them a tree house, which served as their official mystery-solving headquarters. But so far, Frank had never faced an actual bear—and he hoped he never would. He'd seen a show about bears on TV last year. They were huge and could smell people, animals, and food from miles away! Not to mention that when they defended themselves, they stood on their back legs and their fur puffed out so they could look extra big!

Suddenly Frank felt a little queasy. "Dad," he moaned, cradling his stomach with one hand. "I don't feel so good."

"No?" Mr. Hardy said. "What wrong, Frank?"

"He's got FOFT," said Joe, rolling his eyes.

"FOFT?" asked Mr. Hardy.

"Fear of Field Trip," Joe said, cracking a smile in his brother's direction.

"Not that Frank is afraid," said Mrs. Hardy, entering the kitchen. "But you two know that you won't have to see any real bears at Bear Park, right? It's just a silly name." She kissed Frank on the top of his head and handed him a fresh T-shirt, which he swapped out for his soggy one right at the table.

"Or is it?" Joe waggled his eyebrows up and down dramatically.

Even Frank had to laugh at his brother's ridiculous face this time.

"Dad," Frank said, deciding that it was time for a change of subject. "Do you have any cases for work that you need our help with?"

Fenton Hardy was a private detective, and sometimes he worked with the local Bayport Police Department to help solve crimes. When he needed their help, Mr. Hardy was known to tell Frank and Joe about the cases he worked on; he knew the boys had their own detective club and had solved lots of mysteries of their own.

Mr. Hardy showed his sons the front page of the newspaper he was reading. The headline on the front, in big, black letters, read: NY POLICE HUNT FOR JEWEL HEIST ROBBERS!

"A jewel heist!" Joe exclaimed, through a mouthful of Sugar-O's. "Cool!"

"Do you have any leads?" Frank asked seriously.

"A couple," said Mr. Hardy. "While you're on your field trip, I'm going to be at the police station, helping the officers question a suspect."

"Why don't you just arrest him?" asked Joe.

"Because we have to make sure he committed the

crime first," said Mr. Hardy. "Remember last year when Joe thought Mrs. Beasley next door stole his bike?"

Frank laughed, his eyes sparkling. "And we found it the next day, in the backyard. Joe forgot he left it there."

"Honest mistake," Joe defended himself. "She was acting suspicious."

"Exactly," said Mr. Hardy. "But if you'd accused Mrs. Beasley without proof, you'd have looked awfully silly. Same with the jewel heist. Before we arrest someone, we need to have proof he did it, otherwise the real bad guy could get away with robbing that jewelry store."

Frank thought about this for a minute, then took out a pocket notebook that Aunt Trudy had gotten him. Frank and Joe liked to take notes when they were solving a mystery, and this seemed like a very good first note to make in his notebook. *Proof!* he wrote.

"You boys better get a move on," Mrs. Hardy said, pointing at their kitchen clock. "The school bus will be here in ten minutes, and you don't want to miss your field trip."

Frank closed his notebook and placed it in his back pocket. He couldn't help but wonder if missing the field trip was really such a bad thing.

"Watch it, Hardys!" Adam Ackerman, the biggest bully at Bayport Elementary School, pushed past Frank and Joe on his way out of the school bus, stepping on Joe's toes as he went.

They had just arrived at Bayport Bear Park, and Adam was cutting everyone to make sure he was the first one off the bus.

"Even I waited my turn," Cissy Zermeño told Frank and Joe as they climbed down off the school bus. "And I like to be first and best at everything."

Frank and Joe exchanged a look. No one knew how Cissy liked to be number one better than the Hardys. She always won at everything.

"Okay, class," Ms. Potter, one of the chaperones (and a teacher at Bayport Elementary), called out. "Please follow me into the visitors' cabin, single file."

Frank had to admit the park was pretty neat. It

was springtime, so everything was green and bright and the birds were singing their chipper songs. After a long winter, it was nice to see leaves on the trees again, and clover-green grass covered the ground. A few picnic tables and grills for cookouts dotted the park. On the outskirts of the property was a thick, sprawling forest with all different kinds of trees.

That must be where the bears live, thought Frank while a lump formed in his throat.

Straight ahead, Ms. Potter led the line of students into a dark-brown log-cabin-type building. In front of it was a wooden sign that said BAYPORT BEAR PARK VISITORS' CABIN.

Inside the cabin, Joe's classmates were crowded around something that he couldn't see.

"Whoa," said Phil Cohen, one of the Hardys' best friends. "Look at that!"

"What is it?" asked Joe, inching toward the center of the crowd.

That was when Frank and Joe saw it—a big yellow ball about the size and shape of a watermelon, covered in bumblebees!

Looking for another great book?
Find it
IN THE MIDDLE.

Fun, fantastic books for kids
in the in-be**TWEEN** age.

IntheMiddleBooks.com

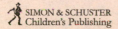
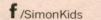

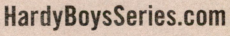

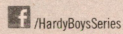